HIS CONVENIENT CURVY BRIDE

IRIS WEST

To you, my reader. I hope you love Garnet City, the sexy men that live there and curvy women they can't help falling helplessly in love with.

CHAPTER ONE

Harper

I MISS MOM. I wish she were here to tell me this is okay. That I'm making the right choice. That marrying Gabriel Cross, one of the richest men in the world, is not a mistake.

I take a deep breath and stare at myself in the mirror, glad that my friend Selena and brother Oscar are both out of the City Hall private waiting room, so I have a few minutes to myself.

I don't recognize the woman there. She's beautiful, like a princess in the fairytales Mom believed in. If only this were a real fairytale, where the bride and the groom are helplessly in love and are marrying to live happily ever after.

However, this is a marriage of convenience. Laughter bubbles up inside of me. I cover my mouth to stop it from coming out. I don't know if I'd be able to stop it.

This whole thing is surreal. I've lived the last couple of weeks, since I said yes to Gabriel's preposterous yet incredibly hard to refuse proposal, in a daze.

Two months ago, when I found out about the new treatment that could drastically improve Oscar's life, I racked my brain for ways to come up with the money. Selena told me about how I could sell my virginity at an auction at The Club for a quarter of a million dollars, but I didn't think I could do it. The idea of sleeping with a total stranger, albeit for one night, was horrendous.

Then last month, Oscar was rushed to the hospital. For the fifth time in as many months. Seeing the excruciating pain in my twenty-year-old brother's face and knowing he would live with pain crisis for the rest of his life, when he didn't have to, changed my mind.

I couldn't bear to see him suffer like that anymore.

I made up my mind and contacted The Club. Had a nerve-racking interview. On the day The Club manager called to give me the okay, Gabriel overheard my conversation. I thought I was alone and asked questions about the night. It was enough to give him a rough idea of what I was planning.

Instead of ignoring the situation or telling me off for talking on the phone at work about private matters like I expected, he'd proposed this marriage.

I shake my head, still finding it hard to believe

Gabriel Cross, the tech mogul, the man who could have any woman on earth, was attracted to me and wanted to marry me. It made little sense then and two weeks later, although I'm dressed in the most beautiful wedding gown I've ever seen and wearing spotless make-up worth thousands of dollars, a part of me still finds this unbelievable.

One day was enough to think about his proposal. For Oscar's sake, I'd wanted to say yes straight away, but I held back. With all the stunning women in the world, I couldn't believe he was attracted to me. Even if he was into curvy women like me, there are prettier women who don't have a brother to care for, for life.

I knew from experience that was a great turn off. My high school sweetheart broke up with me when he realized how much time Oscar would spend with us after Mom and Dad passed. There aren't many men who'd be happy to have a grown brother-in-law live with them forever.

Still, as crazy as it was, what he suggested made more sense than selling my virginity to a stranger.

"People have married for convenience for years. I don't believe in love. I want a partner I find attractive who is sensible and knowledgeable enough to host dinners for those clients who prefer to do business with married people. You want the best medical care for your brother; I can provide that for life. Giving away your virginity will get you a good sum, but it'll be nowhere near enough for the treatment. Even with insurance and subsidies, you'll be short about a million dollars. What will you do to find the rest of the money?" Gabriel had said, in the same tone he used when he was discussing sales reports at meetings.

It was the most I'd ever heard him speak on a topic that wasn't work related in the six months I've been supporting his personal assistant and him.

Even in that moment, my pulse raced. My heart fluttered too, at hearing that the most gorgeous man I'd ever met also found me attractive.

"You're attracted to me now. What if you change your mind before my brother undergoes treatment? Fancy someone else?"

Emerald eyes tracked the length of my body before once again resting on my face.

"That hasn't happened in the two years since you began working for the company."

I'd blinked. Heat spread over my body. My breasts pebbled.

"I don't mess around. Once I decide on something, I stick to it. We'll both sign a contract. One clause is your brother gets lifelong medical care unless you leave."

He'd spelled everything out in the contract. I knew he was the type of man that didn't go back on his decisions. At least not at work. I'd been trying to join his company for years, before I finally got in two years ago.

He kept the pledges he made to his employees. His

company had one of the best employee benefits in the world. More importantly, he didn't care about degrees. All one needed to get in were skills.

I trusted him as a boss. And he was right. I didn't know where I was going to get the rest of the money. So I'd accepted.

But the weight of being married to someone as influential as Gabriel, even with the protection of a contract, scares me.

The door opens. Selena comes in. She takes one look at me and stretches her arms out, as if she's going to hug me. Then pulls back.

"I don't want to ruin your makeup." She takes my hands in hers. "You don't have to do this."

"What about Oscar?"

"I love him to bits, but this is too much. You gave up college, medical school, dating, and your youth to care for him. You're only twenty-four. Giving away your whole life – love and a large family like you've always wanted - isn't fair to you."

"If life were fair, Mom and Dad wouldn't have passed in a senseless accident when I was a freshman. Dad was so proud I was the first child in his family to go to college. He should have lived to see me graduate. And Mom must have worried about Oscar so much." I blink back tears.

"Hey, that's bullshit. She knew you'd take care of him. Besides, remember what she always said?"

"Enjoy today as if it's your last day," we chorus.

"That's why I have to do this," I say.

"That's part of the reason. I hate my brother. Most people are like that. I've never seen someone who doesn't argue with their siblings the way you do. You love Oscar and have always been protective of him."

"If I were younger, I probably would have resented how much time Mom spent taking care of him in hospital and at home. Being four years older changed that. And with him being special, it's hard to hate him."

"I just wish you were marrying for love, like how it should be." She shakes her head. "You're in lust with each other, so who knows? You might fall in love?"

"That mustn't happen. He doesn't want that. I'd be the only one falling. That would be hell."

Oscar comes in.

I look at Selena. She nods and I relax. I don't want my brother to know that my marriage isn't a fairytale. Although he's twenty, his thinking age is only around thirteen.

"Are you ready?" Oscar asks.

I swallow. He looks so handsome in a blue suit that I miss Mom and Dad all over again. I nod.

He puts his arm out, and I place my hand on it.

My jitters calm.

There's a frown on his face that always shows up when he's trying to do his best. He's standing in Dad's place and doesn't want to let him down. It's one reason I love my brother. He always thinks of others.

I'm doing this for him. I'll cope with whatever

comes my way because of him.

We step into the wedding hall, and music plays.

I gaze at Gabriel. His chestnut hair is sleeked back into a trendy style that shows his strong, wide forehead; chiseled nose and cheekbones to perfection. His six-foot-four inches muscular frame is encased in a tailored, dark grey tuxedo that makes him look like a model.

Only, no modelling agency would ever take him because of the scar that runs along the left side of his face. Still, it makes him look more rugged, sexier.

Since I came across his photo six years ago when I was researching his company as a prospective employer, I've been drawn to his looks. Working for him only made that attraction stronger.

When I get close enough to see the expression in his eyes, I can't look away. There's something compelling, magnetic that keeps me trapped in his gaze.

Before I know it, I'm in front of him and Oscar is placing my hand in his. At the contact, my hand tingles.

His eyes widen.

Is he seeing the same desire in mine?

Heat spreads all over my body. My lips feel chapped. I use my tongue to moisten them.

Gabriel glances at my mouth, with eyes darker than I've ever seen them.

My breath hitches.

"Dearly beloved," the Officiant starts.

The hunger disappears from Gabriel's eyes. Suddenly, he's the calm, disciplined boss that leads one of the biggest businesses in the world.

As we turn towards the Officiant, I tell myself to get a grip. I can't control myself the way Gabriel did. No matter how much I'm looking forward to being bedded by him, I must take care to make sure I don't develop feelings for him.

That would lead to misery. If I can keep myself to only feeling lust and respect for him, there's a chance this marriage might bring some kind of contentment. As long as Oscar can stop having painful crises, that would be enough for me.

Thank God our personalities are opposites. There's no way I'll fall in love with a grump.

CHAPTER TWO

Gabriel

I FELL IN lust with Harper the first time I saw her, two years ago. She came up to the executive floor to deliver something to my personal assistant. She was wearing one of the black pencil skirts that seems to be her self-designated uniform and a flowery blouse.

Maybe she thinks those long skirts are conservative, but they stretch over her ass as if they were made just for her. Just thinking about it makes me hard. Which means I'm perpetually hard, since I can't stop thinking about her.

In the last two years, no other woman has made me forget Harper. My cock just isn't interested.

She is the most beautiful woman I've ever seen. Yet,

she's never looked more beautiful that today, in virginal white.

Since she entered the wedding hall, I haven't been able to take my eyes off her. The simple white dress is perfect for her curves.

She tried hard to look strong and happy in front of her brother, but there's a vulnerability in her dark brown eyes, that's endearing.

I try to focus on the Officiant's words. I want every single one of them to be true. For this marriage to be real and bring true happiness.

Until I proposed to Harper, I didn't know how much I wanted to have her permanently in my life.

Oh, I was mad with need for her. There was no other way to describe it apart from obsession. What else would I call the fact that she was on my mind in the morning, at night, and day when I should be thinking about work?

Every time I thought no one was looking, I watched her secretly. I looked up her records, so I'd know as much about her as I could. Six months ago, when she moved up to the executive floor to assist Mrs. Hall and I could see her daily without having to make any excuses to wander to the admin department, my obsession intensified.

The three weeks she covered for my personal assistant, and I had to talk to her, were hell. Because I discovered it wasn't only her body I liked. Her perky voice and bright smile became a new thing to obsess over.

I've liked Mrs. Hall's reserved temperament for years as it matches mine, but suddenly hearing Harper's cheerful voice and watching her smile makes me feel good.

Seeing and hearing her constantly made it impossible to drive her smile and delectable curves away from my mind. Only the strong will I developed over years of hardship and hard work enable me to focus.

However, I didn't realize I wanted to wake up next to her every day of my life. The moment I figured out she was about to give her body to the highest bidder at The Club, I knew. That was only going to happen over my dead body. So, like the negotiator I've become, I put the best terms on the table that would make it impossible for her to refuse my offer.

"Gabriel, do you take Harper Elaine Hamilton to be your lawfully wedded wife from this day forward–to have and to hold, in good times and bad, for richer or poorer, in sickness and in health? Will you love, honor and cherish her for as long as you both shall live?" The Officiant asks.

"I do," I say, meaning the words, as I watch Harper.

She keeps her gaze on me as the Officiant asks her the same question.

"I do."

I release the breath I didn't realize I was holding.

My friend Damon comes forward with the rings.

I'm so nervous, my hands feel heavy as I take Harper's hands and slowly glide her ring over her finger.

She places my ring on my finger, too.

"By the power vested in me by the beautiful state of Arizona, I now pronounce you husband and wife." The officiant smiles at us. "Congratulations. You may kiss the bride."

I watch pink stain Harper's cheeks and my heart races. Something about her innocence drives me wild.

I stare back at her dark brown eyes and cup her cheeks. Slowly, I lower my head until I'm a breath away from her. She closes the gap and our lips touch. It's the most innocent kiss I've ever experienced, yet something inside my chest tightens.

So does my cock.

Loud cheers and claps remind me we're not alone. Gently, I pull back and breathe in and out, trying to control my body and forget that alien feeling in my chest.

As Damon shakes my hand and backslaps me, Selena and Oscar hug Harper.

It's just the five of us and the photographer in the hall, but Selena and Oscar are so loud, it sounds as if there are double the amount of people.

After we sign some paperwork, we take photos inside the hall. Holding Harper feels right. Like she belongs with me. At five feet-eight inches, she fits perfectly under my shoulder but in heels, like she is now, she reaches my shoulder.

"Will the groom please smile down at the bride?" The photographer shouts out after asking me to carry Harper.

"I think Harper is a bit too heavy to carry. Are you okay, Gabriel?" Oscar asks, his face a picture of concern.

I can feel my cheeks heat.

"He has a lot of muscles, Oscar. He's fine," Damon says in a strangled voice.

I want to kill him. I'm almost regretting hiring the photographer, whom he recommended.

I lift my lips. I'm good at many things, smiling is not one of them.

"Just a little wider," the photographer croons, posed at an awkward angle, to get the best shot he can.

"Say cheese," Oscar calls out, trying to help and failing.

I glance at Harper. Her honey skin is flushed, like mine must be.

"We don't have to take it," she says.

Oh, no. We're taking it. I want her to have proper wedding photos.

"I can carry you for another hour," I whisper.

Her skin goes darker. Confusion fills her eyes, making her look cute and sexy simultaneously. Of their own volition, my lips lift.

The camera clicks repeatedly.

"Gorgeous. Gorgeous. All together, now," the photographer says.

We take a few more pictures, then move to the small garden outside. The early summer sun shines brightly on the garden and the photographer insists on taking more photos there.

"It's time to throw the bouquet," Selena says after the photographer leaves.

"You're the only bridesmaid. Here." Harper holds out the flower arrangement, but Selena moves back.

"Throw it," Oscar says.

Harper chuckles. That tight feeling in my chest returns. I stare at the dimples on her cheeks and the tender expression in her eyes. She cares for Oscar and Selena. It's clear in the way her gaze warms whenever she looks at them. Even her voice sounds different when she talks to them.

I want her to look at me that way, too.

"You're smitten. The cold, die hard bachelor has at last fallen." Damon comes up beside me.

I frown. Damon chuckles.

"You really have it bad. You don't even know it. I'd like to be a bee in your house and watch the fun unfurl," he adds.

"What are you up to now?"

I really don't know how we've stayed friends for more than a decade. He spends most of his free time at clubs and parties. Wherever he goes, he's the soul of the party, whilst I'm completely the opposite. My idea of a good time is programming or swimming. But occasionally, we drink together and actually enjoy each other's company.

"You're in love with Harper," Damon whispers.

"Count before you throw it," Oscar laughs.

I watch Harper as she throws the bouquet over her head.

Is wanting her beside me and always needing her to be safe love?

It's not something I'd know. Growing up, I felt little love. The people who took care of me and the other kids in the homes I was raised in did their jobs and went home. Sometimes, there were kind adults who smiled and praised me when I did something good. Most of the time, the workers just didn't care. I preferred it that way.

The kind ones always left. And the other type, the ones who enjoyed hurting kids, never left.

When I was twenty-three, I thought I was in love. Sandra was a socialite. She said she was in love with me, too. But only a few months after we started dating, and I wanted to make things more serious, she admitted to only wanting to know how it felt to sleep with a self-made, scarred man with a shady past. She'd never been with anyone who wasn't flawless. I was good in the sack, she'd said, so she didn't want to break up, but she wanted to make it clear she only wanted the excitement of the unknown.

The small hope growing inside of me I'd at last found love, that despite being abandoned, there was someone who cherished me, was fast extinguished.

I'd rather trust in lust. Of course, I want to protect Harper. I want her safe so I can enjoy her body for the rest of our lives. Taking care of her, her family and making her happy means taking care of me.

It's just like business. I give value to receive value. I want her to trust me the way she trusts Oscar and Selena.

CHAPTER THREE

Harper

WE'RE HEADING TO a small island on the Pacific Ocean in Gabriel's private airplane for a three-day honeymoon. It only takes ten people, but it's as spacious and luxurious as the first-class cabins I've seen on T.V.

I've had so much champagne that I feel tipsy. My idea was to stay sober to make sure I was ready for the first night. However, the friendly flight attendant kept passing by with a filled glass; I couldn't say no.

After City Hall, we all returned to the hotel Oscar, Selena and I stayed at the previous night so I could change then we had lunch at a famous restaurant, the three of us had hoped to eat at for a while, since Oscar heard they did the best steak in Arizona a few years ago.

Saying goodbye to him was heart-wrenching. Apart

from the few weeks I was in college, we've never spent a night away from each other. He would love to be here, but taking him wouldn't have been fair to Gabriel.

He looks up from the report he was reading.

"Are you missing your brother?"

"How did you know?"

"You have this expression when you look at him. Your eyes look the same way you did earlier, when you were speaking with him."

"It'll pass. He'll be happy enough at home with Selena." She'd offered to stay at our house with him. We were moving to Gabriel's house only after the honeymoon.

"If we need to get back, it'll only take a couple of hours. The pilot is on standby."

Warmth spreads in my heart as I look at him. From the moment I signed the marriage contract, he's been referring to me, Oscar, and him as us. It makes me feel like he's already taking responsibility for us as a family. For six years, since Mom and Dad's accident, I've made all decisions and taken care of everything in our lives. It's strange, yet reassuring, to know that I'm no longer alone.

"Thank you!"

I turn and gaze at the white mass of clouds outside the window so he doesn't see how emotional I'm being. As well as being a great employer, I suspected he was a caring man. He offers scholarships to talented young people all over the world. Plus, he donates to several charities. Some people might say that's okay since he doesn't have children to leave his fortune to.

However, I believe he genuinely wants to help people.

The pilot explains we're going to land and Gabriel puts his papers away.

"Did you finish revising the urgent paperwork?"

He gazes at me.

"I did. I'm all yours now."

I cough. A blush spreads over my neck and face.

Gabriel grins.

It transforms his face. Makes his expression open, more approachable.

"When you smile, you look really boyish. Sexier than usual."

"Sexier than usual, eh? I like that."

That's when I realize I spoke aloud.

I turn to the window again, this time deciding to avert my face from him until I've sobered up. But not before I noticed how cute he is when he jokes.

In the six months I worked for his assistant and while I was covering for her, not once did I see him joke. He rarely smiles. Whether it's with his department managers when he's in meetings, or Mrs. Hall with whom he has worked for over a decade or in the rare magazine interview, he accepts.

When we arrive at the island, it's late afternoon. I follow Gabriel to a brand-new truck parked near the landing strip. He has a distinctive gait, caused by a shorter leg, which I can't help thinking adds to his rugged sex appeal.

"You leave it unlocked? What if someone steals it?" I ask after he ushers me into the truck.

"Only the caretakers and the pilot come here. It's private land."

"So, we and the caretakers are the only people on the island?"

Gabriel drives off in the sand. I stare at the aquamarine sea and clear blue sky. A seagull takes flight near the edge of the water, it's singing loud in the quiet. It's paradise.

"They'll leave for the main island once I introduce you to them."

So, it'll be just the two of us. I try not to be intimidated by Gabriel's wealth, but when the house we're staying in comes into view; I gasp. It's unlike anything I've ever seen.

"Your house is beautiful."

"Our house, Harper."

I nod. It'll take substantially more than the few hours we've been married for me to think of his houses as ours.

"This is my wife, Mrs. Cross," Gabriel says to the family of five that greets us outside the house.

"Please call if there's anything you need," the housekeeper, Mrs. Baton, says.

I watch her, her husband, and three grown children

walk away.

"How long have they worked for you?"

"Since I bought the island eleven years ago. They helped with building the house and managed the construction."

Gabriel takes me on a tour of the three-bedroom house.

"This is our bedroom."

My gaze strays to the massive bed. When I glance at him, he's staring at me. I check out the bathroom, telling myself to stop thinking dirty. The large tub, big enough to fit two people, doesn't help.

I avoid Gabriel's eyes as I escape to another room in the house.

"This can be Oscar's bedroom," he says.

A lump forms in my throat. At this rate, not falling in love with him will be extremely hard.

After putting our bags away, we stuff two plates with food Mrs. Baton prepared and take a bottle of wine outside. We have dinner on the beach watching the sunset. The orange glow on the horizon is so beautiful, it takes my breath away.

"You must have been under twenty-five when you bought this island. Was that a dream you had?"

Gabriel is silent for so long, I think he will not answer.

"I grew up in a home. When I was about twelve, it was declared too old to maintain safely, so I moved to another home. There was little privacy. So, kind of. I promised myself that when I made enough money, I'd get a place where I could stay by myself whenever I wanted."

I can't imagine being alone for long periods of time. My parents have always been around me. Even if we weren't in the same room, I liked knowing someone was in the house.

Gabriel must enjoy being on his own. At work, he doesn't go out with the other workers like the managers do. He eats alone, at his desk.

"What's the longest you stayed here by yourself?"

"One month. It's hard to get away for longer than that."

"You were only nineteen when you sold your first computer program and became a millionaire. You must have worked hard all your teenage years. You still do. Don't you get tired and want to give it all up and retire?" I've always wanted to know.

He was the first to arrive at work and the last to leave. I've always felt a little sad seeing him slog like that, especially during the holidays.

"I love programming. It's my work and hobby." He takes a sip of wine, then looks at me. "I ran away from my home when I was sixteen. I caught one worker abusing a young boy." He shrugs.

"I suppose I should have ignored it, but I couldn't. The staff member tried to intimidate me into being quiet, but I fought back. That's how I got the scar."

"You must have been terrified!" What horrors did

he go through?

He shrugs again and my heart breaks a little for the boy he must have been.

"It was life. The kid refused to testify, but there were signs of abuse on him, so the staff member was arrested. Since then, the carers looked at me differently. So did the other kids. I figured I'd be better off on my own and left. So, while most other kids my age were going to school, I was developing my own programs. When I turned eighteen, I sold them."

In the semi-darkness, he looks awkward, making me wonder if he's ever talked about this before. There's nothing about it in the interviews he's done. It's common knowledge he's a high school drop-out and took the GED when he was eighteen, but not the reason.

"No wonder you're an inspiration to young people across the globe. I was gutted when my parents passed and I had to drop out of school to care for Oscar. Coming across your company and it's policy to hire anyone with the right skills regardless of education level, gave me hope. I decided then and there I was going to work at Cross Tech. Your story inspired me."

"I'm glad," he says, his voice thick like molasses.

"Thank you for telling me your story."

"I want you to know the real me. Being honest with each other will help our family and marriage."

The more time I spend in his company, the more I appreciate his idea of a good marriage. It's not perfect;

I don't think a relationship can ever be great without love. Yet, being honest with each other will make our relationship, whatever it is, better.

Still, can a clause in a contract really solve all problems? There's no way I can tell him to stop treating Oscar as family because his care and attention is already making me fall a little in love with him.

CHAPTER FOUR

Gabriel

I SWIM MY twentieth lap and get out of the sea. The water is warm, and the sun beats down on my back. I stare at the sky, enjoying the fresh air and the smell of the sea. When I reach the large mat spread on the beach, under an enormous umbrella, I grab a towel and rub myself dry.

I head back to the house, wondering if Harper is awake. Yet, as soon as I walk in, I sense the quiet of the house. I pad to the bedroom, careful not to wake her. She's sleeping on her front, with her arms crossed on the pillow; her head lying on them.

She's always busy doing something or another; it's strange to see her so still. I'm tempted to step in farther and examine the bow of her mouth, little upturned nose and arched eyebrows, but I don't want to wake her.

I move to the kitchen and get breakfast ready. There's bacon and sausages in the refrigerator so I warm them up and fry eggs, sunny side up, making a note to ask how she likes them.

I remember telling her about how I got my scar and I grimace. I've never told anyone about that. It was hard and cringy, yet I wanted her to know about my life.

Footsteps sound in the hallway.

"Good morning," she says.

"Did you sleep well?"

"Sorry, I fell asleep on you last night. Too much champagne, wine and fresh air."

I didn't want to wake her, so I carried her inside and put her to bed.

She looks around the massive kitchen and heads for a cabinet; pulls out the drawers and removes cutlery; places it on the table.

"Bacon, eggs, and sausages, okay?"

"It is, and it smells wonderful. Let me make breakfast tomorrow."

"We can do it together. Mrs. Baton did most of this, I just reheated it."

"What time did you wake up?" She asks after we start eating.

"At sunrise. It's a habit. I watched the sunrise and swam."

"Do you swim every day? You always stay at a hotel with a swimming pool when you travel."

"It's another habit. It helps to keep my leg strong."

Harper hesitates.

I hate answering questions about my personal life. It's part of the reason I don't have many friends. The idea of opening up about my life is uncomfortable. Why do I find her curiosity cute?

"It's okay. Ask."

"Does it hurt? Your leg?"

"Rarely, if I hike for long periods of time, like six hours or more. That's why I swim, it puts less pressure on it. I was born with it; I've learnt to live with it. So, there's no problem with carrying you."

She looks out the window.

"I can't believe you're still teasing me about that photo incident."

A smile hovers around her lips.

"It turns out I enjoy teasing you."

Harper blushes.

"I'll wash up." She gathers crockery.

I clear the table and wash up with her.

"What are we doing today?"

"We can swim and snorkel or go shopping on the main island."

"Swimming and snorkeling sound wonderful. If you're okay with it."

I leave her to change while I get the snorkeling equipment from the shed.

"Do you have much experience with snorkeling?" I ask when she comes outside. I busy myself putting on my gear to stop ogling the curves barely hidden by her bikini.

"My parents couldn't afford fancy holidays. Every summer, we'd load up our car with groceries and travel around. Most of the time we camped in woodlands but sometimes, we'd go to the sea. Snorkeling didn't cost any money, so we did that and swam a lot."

We swim leisurely towards the ocean. I stop her when I spot a place we can explore. We spend a couple of hours checking out the marine life and are lucky enough to spot a turtle.

Back on the beach, we dry up and sit on the beach mat, watching the sea as we down iced lemonade from the cool box I brought out earlier.

"Are you hungry?" I ask.

"Not yet."

Beads of water fall from her black, tightly curled hair to the bare honey skin of her shoulders. The need to taste that tempting skin rises, making me salivate.

I reach across and chase a drop with a finger down her back, until I reach the top of her white bikini, which soaks up the drop.

Harper shivers.

"Cold?"

I glance at her face. Dilated, dark brown eyes meet mine.

A pink tongue moistens soft, nude lips.

"No," she whispers.

I trail my finger up her back, past the tie of her

bikini, and trace the delicate curve of her neck. She shivers under my touch, her satiny skin erupting in goosebumps despite the heat of the tropical sun beating down on us.

I can't tear my gaze away from her. In her tiny bikini, she's all lush curves and honey skin that begs to be touched, tasted, worshipped. My eyes lock onto hers, the air between us crackling with the force of our mutual desire.

"Harper." Her name falls from my lips like a reverent prayer.

Then I'm kissing her, hot and urgent and deep. She melts into me with a soft moan that sets my blood on fire, her lips parting to welcome the sweep of my tongue. She tastes of strawberries and sunshine and something uniquely Harper. Sweet, addictive, and intoxicating.

She twines her arms around my neck, pressing the soft swells of her breasts against the hard planes of my chest as if she can't get close enough. I want to burrow under her skin, to sink so deep inside her warmth that we fuse into one perfect being.

Without breaking the kiss, I lower us onto the warm beach mat.

My hands roam greedily over her silken flesh as I strip away her bikini top, desperate to feel every inch of her. Her full breasts spill into my palms, the dusky nipples pebbling against my roughened skin. I dip my head to take one into my mouth, swirling my tongue around the sensitive peak before drawing on it firmly.

Harper arches beneath me, a moan falling from her kiss-swollen lips. "Gabriel, please..."

"Please what, baby?"

My lips trail wet, open-mouthed kisses along the slender column of her throat. Her pulse hammers wildly beneath my tongue and it sends a thrill of masculine pride through me, knowing the effect I have on her.

"Tell me what you need."

"You," she gasps as I find that sweet spot just below her ear that makes her shudder. "I need you, Gabriel."

CHAPTER FIVE

Gabriel

I LIFT MY head to gaze down at her, my heart clenching almost painfully in my chest at the raw desire shimmering in the depths of her chocolate eyes. "You have me, Harper. I'm yours."

My voice is gruff, roughened by the sheer intensity of my need for this woman. I've wanted no one the way I want her. It's a hunger that goes beyond the physical, a soul-deep yearning I can feel etched into my very marrow.

Harper cups my face in her hands, her thumbs grazing my beard.

"Then make me yours, Gabriel."

A guttural growl rumbles up from my chest as I claim her lips again in a searing kiss. My fingers find the ties of her bikini bottoms and yank impatiently, baring her completely to my ravenous gaze. She's breathtaking like this, all curvaceous limbs and smooth olive skin and a delectable little thatch of black curls at the apex of her thighs that beckons me.

I blaze a trail of hot, open-mouthed kisses down her throat, over her breasts, to the sensitive skin of her ribs and soft belly. I dip my tongue into her navel, swirling, teasing, smiling against her skin when she squirms restlessly beneath me. My hands stroke slowly up the silken skin of her inner thighs, urging them gently apart.

"You smell incredible," I groan, nuzzling my face into her damp curls. "I bet you taste even sweeter."

Harper mewls softly, her hips lifting in shameless invitation. Keeping my eyes locked on hers, I part her glistening folds with the pads of my thumbs, revealing the slick pink flesh that weeps with her arousal.

I take a moment to admire the sight of her laid out before me like a feast, her pussy flushed and glistening with need. Need for me. It's humbling and sexy all at once.

I lean in and drag the flat of my tongue along her slit, a guttural moan vibrating up from my chest at that first exquisite taste of her essence bursting across my taste buds. She's honey and spice and something that is all her.

"Gabriel!" she cries out sharply, her fingers sinking into my hair, holding me to her as I feast.

I take my time, exploring every silken fold, every secret hollow with lips and tongue until she's writhing beneath me, her breath coming in shallow pants. I spear my tongue inside her tight channel, and I lap at her walls, reveling in the way she thrashes beneath me, wanton and unrestrained.

I feel her tightening, her thighs quivering as I work her closer to the edge. I replace my tongue with a finger and wrap my lips around the sensitive bundle of nerves at the top of her sex and suckle gently, flicking the tip of my tongue rapidly against the swollen flesh.

Harper shatters with a hoarse cry, her fingers clenching almost painfully in my hair as her release crashes over her. I work her through it with gentle strokes of my tongue and finger, prolonging her pleasure until she collapses back onto the mat, spent and trembling.

I press a final, reverent kiss to her intimate flesh before crawling up her body to take her mouth in a deep, drugging kiss.

Harper moans, her arms coming up to wind around my neck, holding me close.

"You are so damn beautiful. So perfect. I can't believe that you're really mine."

"I am yours, Gabriel. I've never felt like this before. Wanted no one the way I want you."

I have to close my eyes against the sudden swell of emotion burning in my chest - a feeling so intense, so all-consuming I don't have a name for it. All I know is that this woman, this ray of sunshine who burst into my life and lit up all the dark corners of my soul, is everything to me.

"Me too. You're in my blood, Harper. You've ruined me for anyone else."

Her breath hitches, her eyes going wide and liquid with an emotion that steals the air from my lungs. She says nothing, just pulls me down into a kiss that feels like a promise, a silent avowal.

I settle myself between her thighs, the hard length of my cock nestling into her slick heat. But as much as I'm dying to bury myself inside her, to claim her in the most primal way imaginable, I force myself to slow down.

I'll be her first man. The thought fills me with a sense of possessive pride - that I get to be the one to show her this pleasure, to worship her body the way it deserves. But it also sobers me, reminds me I need to be careful with her, gentle. The last thing I want is to hurt her.

"We'll go slow," I promise as I position myself at her entrance. "If it's too much, if you need me to stop, tell me. Okay?"

Her fingers dig into the muscles of my shoulders.

"I want this. I want you."

Holding her gaze, I push forward, gritting my teeth at the feel of her body stretched impossibly tight around me. Harper tenses, her face pinching and I freeze instantly.

"Breathe, baby." I brush featherlight kisses over her cheeks, her eyelids, the tip of her nose. "Try to relax for me. I've got you."

She exhales shakily and I feel her consciously relax around me, her tight sheath easing just a fraction. I kiss her as I rock my hips shallowly, working myself progressively deeper, letting her adjust to the unfamiliar stretch and fullness.

When I'm finally fully inside of her, we both release a shuddering breath. I drop my forehead to hers, my heart hammering against my ribs as I fight the urge to move, to take. She feels too good, hot and tight and perfect, her slick walls gripping me like a velvet fist.

"Are you alright? Do you need a minute?"

She rolls her hips into mine. The movement sends sparks of pleasure shooting up my spine, making me groan.

"I'm okay. I feel... full. But it's good. You feel good."

I have to kiss her for that, my tongue delving into her mouth in an electrifying slide as I begin to move. I start slow, easing out and then gliding back in with shallow strokes as she grows accustomed to the feel of me inside her. But soon she's arching into me, her hips rising to meet my every thrust, and I know she's ready for more.

I pick up the pace gradually, rolling my hips into hers harder, deeper, our flesh coming together in a slap that mingles with our ragged breathing and the distant crash of the waves.

Harper clings to me as I claim her body over and over, her head thrown back, the elegant line of her throat bared to my hungry mouth. I can't resist the temptation, fastening my lips to her racing pulse as my thrusts grow faster, more urgent.

I can feel the tension coiling tighter at the base of my spine, my release barreling down on me. However, I clench my jaw and hold it at bay through sheer force of will, determined to bring Harper over with me. I want to feel her come apart in my arms, to hear her cry out my name in ecstasy as I fill her with my seed.

I wedge a hand between our writhing bodies, finding her clit. I stroke it with firm, purposeful circles, keeping tempo with the relentless pistoning of my hips.

Harper keens, her fingers scrabbling over my sweat-slicked back, her breath coming in high, thin pants as I drive her towards the edge. "Gabriel, I... I'm close. I'm so close."

"Let go, baby," I urge her, my voice guttural and wrecked, barely recognizable to my own ears. "I've got you. Let go for me."

I grind against her, hitting a spot deep inside that has her body locking up, taut as a tripwire. Her mouth falls open on a soundless cry and then she's shattering in my arms, clenching down on me rhythmically as wave after wave of sensation crashes over her.

The feel of her coming undone around me is too much to withstand. With a hoarse shout, I follow her over, my release slamming into me with the force of a tidal wave. I bury my face in the sweat-damp curve of her throat as I empty myself inside her, my hips churning mindlessly as the most intense pleasure I've ever known burns through my veins.

It seems to go on forever; the world narrowing down to this single perfect moment, our bodies joined so intimately, moving as one. I've never felt so connected to another person, so completely in sync.

Long moments later, I collapse against her, taking care to keep the bulk of my weight braced on my elbows. We're both panting, our skin flushed and damp.

Harper runs soothing hands up and down my back, her touch grounding me even as aftershocks continue to roll through me.

When I finally find the strength to lift my head, it's to find Harper watching me with a soft, wondering expression on her beautiful face. Her chocolate eyes are liquid and luminous, filled with a tender emotion that makes my throat tighten and my chest ache.

"That was..." she trails off, shaking her head as if at a loss for words.

"Incredible," I finish for her, my voice raw and raspy. "Earth-shattering. The best damn thing I've ever felt in my life."

A shy smile tugs at her kiss-swollen lips. "For me too. I didn't know it could be like that. So intense."

I brush a thumb over the apple of her cheek, marveling at the way she leans into my touch, as if craving the contact.

"It's never been like that for me either, Harper. You're special. This thing between us...it's special. And I promise you, I'm going to spend every day showing you how good we can be together."

Her breath hitches, her eyes going wide and shimmery with emotion. "Gabriel..."

I silence her with a soft, lingering kiss. "You don't have to say anything. I just need you to know that I'm in this marriage for good. You're it for me, Harper."

She makes a sound halfway between a laugh and a sob, wrapping her arms around me and holding on tight. I gather her close, pressing my lips to her temple as I breathe in the warm honey scent of her skin.

In this moment, with Harper safe and sated in my embrace, the future stretching out before us ripe with promise; I feel a sense of peace, of rightness, I've never known before.

And it's all because of the incredible woman in my arms.

My Harper.

Mine.

CHAPTER SIX

Harper

I SIT IN the plush living room of Gabriel's sprawling mansion, waiting for him and Oscar to come play Twister. It's become a nightly ritual, a way for us to bond as a family. Family. The word sends a pang of longing through my chest.

It's been three weeks since I moved in, three weeks of adjusting to this new life as Mrs. Cross. Sometimes it still feels surreal, like I'm living someone else's fairytale. The luxurious furnishings, the attentive staff, the sheer opulence of everything - it's a far cry from our cozy, lovely yet old home.

But it's more than just the material comforts. It's the sense of belonging, of safety. For the first time since our parents died, I feel like Oscar and I have a stable home. A place where we're cherished, protected, and I'm not stressed out of my mind worrying about bills.

And so much of that is because of Gabriel.

I lean back against the sofa cushions, a wistful smile tugging at my lips as my mind drifts to our honeymoon. After that first explosive encounter on the beach, we barely left the bedroom. We made love repeatedly, mapping each other's bodies with hands and lips and tongues, learning every secret place that made the other gasp and moan.

It was more than just physical pleasure, though. In those moments, tangled up in the sheets with the hot press of Gabriel's skin against mine, I felt a connection I've never experienced before. A sense of rightness.

But I can't let myself dwell on that, on the fragile hope that whispers maybe, just maybe, he feels it too. I know the terms of our agreement. No love, no children. Just a mutually beneficial arrangement.

I signed that contract with eyes wide open, knowing full well what I was giving up. I didn't have a choice. Oscar's mounting medical bills, his need for that experimental treatment...I would have done anything to save my brother.

And I don't regret it, even now. Because Oscar's treatment is scheduled for five weeks from now. And Gabriel has been so good to us. Better than I ever could have hoped.

In the weeks since we returned to Garnet City, we've settled into a comfortable routine. Gabriel goes to work during the day but is home in time for dinner, which makes my heart swell with gratitude. He listens attentively as Oscar chatters about his day at the community center or his latest doctor's appointment, asking questions and offering encouragement in equal measure.

I'm even enjoying my new role as Gabriel's wife, at least in the public eye. We hosted a dinner party last week for some of his business associates and I couldn't help the thrill that went through me every time he introduced me as "Mrs. Cross". The pride in his voice, the possessive hand at the small of my back...it made me feel cherished. Adored.

But I have to be careful. I can't let myself read too much into his actions, his words. Can't let myself believe that the way he looks at me when we're making love means anything more than physical desire.

We have a good life, a comfortable one. If I let myself fall any deeper, let myself hope for the impossible... I risk losing everything. And I won't do that to Oscar. I won't upend his world again, not when he's finally found stability and happiness.

If that means living with a half-full heart and never knowing the joy of cradling my child in my arms, so be it.

Shaking off my thoughts, I glance at the clock on the mantel. What's taking Gabriel and Oscar so long? I push to my feet and make my way towards Oscar's room, figuring they might have gotten distracted by one of his video games again.

But as I approach the partially open door, I hear the low rumble of Gabriel's voice, uncharacteristically gentle. Concerned. I pause, not wanting to interrupt.

"You were quieter than usual at dinner tonight, buddy," Gabriel is saying. "Everything okay?"

There's a beat of silence before Oscar answers, his voice small and unsure. "Someone at the community center...he called me stupid. Said I wasn't normal." He sniffles and my heart cracks in my chest. "I didn't want to tell Harper. She gets sad when people say mean stuff like that."

"Oh, Oscar." The sorrow in Gabriel's voice, the tender understanding...it brings tears to my eyes. "I'm so sorry that happened. But you know he's wrong, right? You're not stupid. You're brilliant, in your own special way."

"I am?" Oscar sounds so painfully hopeful, so desperate for reassurance.

"Absolutely." Gabriel's voice is firm, almost fierce. "You see the world differently than most people. You find joy in little things, things others take for granted. That's a gift. A superpower."

"Like your leg?" Oscar asks, curious. "Harper said you're special too, 'cause you have a shorter leg."

Gabriel chuckles, but there's an edge of old pain to the sound that makes my chest ache. "Yeah, like my leg. I know what it feels like to be different, Oscar. To have people look at you and see someone defective or broken. But that doesn't make it true."

"It doesn't?"

"Not even a little. We're exactly who we're meant to be. And the people who really care for us? They see that. They celebrate it." Gabriel clears his throat, his voice going gruff with emotion. "I never had that growing up. Never had a mom or dad to tell me I was special, that I mattered. But I'm telling you now, Oscar. You matter. You're important and loved, just as you are."

Tears are sliding down my cheeks now, my heart so full it feels like it might burst. In that moment, listening to Gabriel comfort my brother with such genuine care and affection, I realize the truth I've been denying for weeks.

I'm in love with him. Desperately, irrevocably in love.

The knowledge crashes over me, stealing my breath and sending my pulse racing. I love him. I love his strength and his gentleness, his brilliant mind and his wounded heart. I love the way he's opened himself up to Oscar and me, the way he's let us into his life and his home without reservation.

But I can't tell him. I can't risk shattering the fragile peace we've found, jeopardizing Oscar's chance at a healthy future. He was clear about the terms of our marriage. If he finds out how I feel...it could ruin everything.

So I'll lock my feelings away. I'll content myself with the care he gives me, the moments of tenderness I can pretend mean more than they do. It's enough. It has to be.

Drawing in a shaky breath, I paste on a bright smile and push into the room. "There you are! I was thinking you'd forgotten about our game night."

Oscar jumps up from where he's sitting cross-legged on the floor, his face lighting up. "Twister time! I call dibs on green!"

Gabriel stands more slowly, his eyes finding mine. For a moment, I'm terrified he'll see the truth written all over my face, but he just smiles, soft and intimate. "Guess that leaves red for me and blue for you, baby."

Baby. The endearment rolls off his tongue so easily now, but it still makes my stomach flip every time. If only it meant what I long for it to mean...

But I shove that thought away, determined to enjoy this time with my two of my favorite people. We make our way to the living room, Oscar chattering excitedly as he sets up the game mat.

"Left hand red!" Oscar announces gleefully after spinning the wheel.

We all comply, bending and stretching to reach our circles. It doesn't take long before we're a tangled mess of limbs, giggling breathlessly as we try to maintain our balance.

"Right foot yellow," Gabriel grunts, his face inches from mine as he arches over me to reach his dot. His breath fans across my cheek and I fight back a shiver, my skin prickling with awareness.

"Careful there, mister," I tease, trying to ignore the

way my heart stutters at his proximity. "No cheating allowed!"

Gabriel flashes me a playful grin, his green eyes sparkling with mirth. "Wouldn't dream of it. I'm just naturally flexible."

I snort out a laugh, nearly losing my balance in the process. "Is that so? Well, let's see how flexible you are when I do... this!"

I bump my hip against his, trying to knock him off balance. He wobbles precariously for a moment before righting himself, his low chuckle sending warmth coursing through my veins.

"Oh, it's on now," he growls, retaliating with a gentle nudge of his own. "Two can play at that game!"

We dissolve into laughter, our competitive sides coming out as we try to one-up each other. Oscar eggs us on from his spot on the mat, his face split in a wide, delighted grin.

"Go Harper! No, go Gabriel! Wait, no... go, both of you!"

His enthusiasm is infectious and soon we're all laughing so hard we can barely keep our positions. It's the simple happiness I've always yearned for.

"Left foot blue!" Oscar calls out, still giggling.

I stretch my leg out, trying to reach the blue dot. But my sock slips on the plastic mat and I go down in a tangle of limbs, pulling Gabriel with me. We land in a breathless heap, his solid weight pressing me onto the floor.

For a while, we just stare at each other, caught in the unexpected intimacy of the moment. His eyes are soft and warm, his smile tender as he reaches out to brush a strand of hair from my forehead.

"You okay there, klutz?" he murmurs, his voice low and teasing.

I stick my tongue out at him, trying to ignore the way my heart is pounding. "I meant to do that. It's called strategic losing."

"Is that what we're calling it now?" He grins, the corners of his eyes crinkling in the way I adore. "Guess that means Oscar wins by default."

"Yes!" Oscar pumps his fist in the air, his face flushed with excitement. "I'm the Twister champion!"

Gabriel levers himself up and off me, holding out a hand to help me to my feet. I take it, trying not to dwell on how perfectly our palms fit together, how right it feels to have his fingers laced with mine.

"What do you say, champ?" Gabriel asks, slinging an arm around Oscar's shoulders. "Ready for round two?"

Oscar nods eagerly, already scrambling to reset the game board. "You bet! But no more strategic losing, okay Harper?"

I hold up my hands in mock surrender, fighting back a grin. "Scout's honor, little bro. This time I'm playing to win!"

Gabriel shoots me a wink, his expression playful and full of warmth. "Bring it on. Loser makes hot cocoa after?"

"Oh, you are so on." I rub my hands together in anticipation, feeling lighter than I have in weeks.

This. This is what I want to hold on to. These perfect, shining moments of laughter and love, of feeling like we truly belong to each other. Even if it's not in the way my heart longs for, even if I have to content myself with friendship instead of passion...it's enough.

So I let myself get swept up in the game, in the easy affection and playful trash talk. I let myself savor every smile, every casual touch and shared joke. And for a little while, I let myself forget about contracts and rules, about the impossible yearnings of my foolish heart.

CHAPTER SEVEN

Harper

I SIT AT a corner table in Amalia's Place, nervously fiddling with the straw in my untouched iced tea. The trendy downtown pub is bustling with the usual Friday night crowd, but I barely notice the chatter and laughter surrounding me. My mind is a million miles away, lost in a haze of fear and uncertainty.

I glance down at my phone, checking the time for the hundredth time. Selena should be here any minute. I need her now more than ever, need her steady presence and unwavering support. Because my world has just been turned upside down in the most unexpected way.

I'm pregnant. Five weeks along, according to the doctor I saw this morning. And not just one baby, but three. Triplets. The word echoes in my head, a dizzying refrain that still doesn't feel real.

I should have known something was off when I missed my period. I'm usually like clockwork, but with everything going on - Oscar's pre-treatments, tests and appointments; settling into life with Gabriel - I didn't think much of it at first. But then the nausea started.

Three pregnancy tests later, all positive, and I knew I needed to see a doctor. To confirm what my heart already knew to be true. But hearing it out loud, seeing the tiny flickering heartbeats on the ultrasound screen...it made it real in a way I wasn't prepared for.

I rest a hand on my still-flat stomach, a fierce surge of protectiveness rushing through me. These babies...they're a part of me. A part of Gabriel. Created out of the love and passion we've shared, even if he doesn't know it yet.

And that's the problem, isn't it? Gabriel doesn't want this. If I go through with this pregnancy, if I choose these babies...I risk losing everything.

Losing Gabriel. Losing the happy, stable life we've built together. The laughter and warmth and sense of belonging that's become as necessary to me as air. And worst of all, losing the financial support that's paying for the treatment that can rid Oscar of the pain inducing, abnormally shaped red blood cells in his body.

The thought makes bile rise in my throat, tears burning behind my eyes. How can I choose between my babies and my brother?

But even as my mind races with worst-case scenarios, I know deep down that I can't give up these babies. They're a miracle, a gift I never thought I'd have. And I already love them with a ferocity that takes my breath away.

"Harper!"

Selena's voice snaps me out of my spiraling thoughts. She weaves her way through the crowded bar, her face etched with concern as she slides into the booth across from me.

"Hey sweetie, sorry I'm late. Traffic was a nightmare." She reaches across the table to squeeze my hand, her brow furrowed. "What's going on? You sounded strange on the phone, scared me half to death."

"I didn't mean to worry you."

Selena searches my face, her expression softening.

"Spill - what's got you looking like you've seen a ghost?"

I take a deep breath, steeling myself. I'd planned on telling her everything, blurting out my news and begging for her advice. But now, sitting here with the words on the tip of my tongue, I hesitate.

Gabriel deserves to know first. He's the father. I owe him the respect of hearing it from me before anyone else.

So I swallow down the confession, forcing my racing thoughts in a different direction.

"It's Gabriel," I say instead, my voice small and

strained. "I'm in love with him, Selena. Like, head-over-heels, can't-imagine-my-life-without-him in love. And I'm terrified."

Selena sits back, her eyes wide. "Oh, Harper. That's huge."

"I don't know what to do. We had a deal, an arrangement. But I broke the rules. I fell for him anyway."

"Are you sure he doesn't feel the same way?" Selena asks gently. "The way he looks at you, the way he is with Oscar, that's not just friendship. That's real."

"I don't know. Sometimes I think maybe, but then I remember the contract. The way he was so adamant about not wanting love, not wanting kids. Why would he put that in there if he was open to more?"

Selena is quiet for a long moment, her gaze thoughtful. "I think," she says slowly, "that Gabriel might be more afraid of love than opposed to it. Think about it, Harper. With all the women in the world who have baggage, who come with complications, why did he choose you?"

"I don't know. Convenience, maybe? I was already his assistant, already knew him."

But even as I say it, I know it's not the full truth. Selena seems to know it too, because she shakes her head.

"Gabriel has owned his company for over fifteen years, Harper. I guarantee you're not the first beautiful assistant he's had in that time. Not the first single woman with responsibilities who's crossed his path. But you're the one he offered this deal to. The one he married."

I sit with that for a moment, hardly daring to hope. Could she be right? Could there be more to his feelings?

"He has changed since the wedding. He's softer, more open and affectionate, not just with me, but with Oscar, too. It's like he's letting himself care. Letting himself be part of a family."

"Exactly. Men like Gabriel don't do that for just anyone, Harper. He might not be ready to admit it, even to himself, but that man is falling for you. Hard."

A thrill goes through me at her words, followed quickly by a crush of panic. If she's right, if Gabriel really has feelings for me...how will he react to the pregnancy? Will it send him running, reinforcing all his fears about love and commitment? Or will it be the catalyst that finally breaks down his walls, that shows him the beauty of the future we could have together?

"What do I do, Selena? I'm so scared of losing him. Of losing everything we've fought so hard to build. But I can't keep going like this, can't keep hiding how I feel. It's eating me alive."

Selena reaches out again, her hand warm and steady over mine. "Oh Harper. I wish I had all the answers. But this is between you and Gabriel. You need to talk to him, need to lay it all out on the table. The feelings, the fears, all of it."

"I know you're right. I just think I need a little time.

To wrap my head around it, figure out what I want to say. How I want to say it."

"Take all the time you need. But don't wait too long, okay? You both deserve happiness. I think you could have that, if you're brave enough to reach for it."

Tears sting my eyes at her fierce sincerity and unwavering faith that hasn't changed since kindergarten. "Thank you. For being the best friend a girl could ask for."

Selena smiles, her own eyes suspiciously misty. "You started it when you punched Billy after he called me fat. You're stuck with me."

A watery laugh escapes me.

We sit in comfortable silence for a moment, sipping our drinks and letting the conversation settle. My mind is still whirling, still grappling with the enormity of the secrets I'm keeping. But there's a glimmer of hope now too, a flicker of possibility amidst the fear.

"I'm going to tell him," I say quietly, decisively. "Not tonight, not yet. I need a little more time. But soon. I'll ask him to have dinner with me, somewhere quiet where we can really talk. And I'll tell him everything."

"Good. I know it won't be easy. But you're doing the right thing."

I'll just have to find a way to make it work. To convince Gabriel to let me keep the babies, lend me money to continue Oscar's treatments. I'll promise to raise them on my own, to never ask for anything more from him. I'll spend the rest of my life paying him back the money for the money for Oscar's treatment.

The thought of facing the future without him is too painful to bear.

But I know now, with bone-deep certainty, that I'll bear it if I have to. For my babies, for the tiny lives depending on me, I'll find the strength to do this. With or without Gabriel by my side.

I just pray that it's with him. That the love I feel for him is enough to overcome every obstacle, fear and doubt.

That it's enough to build a life on, a real happily ever after, beyond the pages of any contract.

But for now, for tonight...I let myself lean on my best friend. I let myself be scared and hopeful and everything in between.

CHAPTER EIGHT

Gabriel

SOMETHING IS WRONG. I felt it in the unnatural stillness of the house, the absence of Harper's usual cheerful humming as I stepped through the door after work.

I shake my head as I brush my teeth, using more force than necessary.

The past few days, she's been different. Our lovemaking has been more urgent, almost desperate, as if she's trying to pour whatever she can't say into the press of her body against mine. It's like she's slipping through my fingers, and I'm terrified of what it means.

Terrified that she's tired of me, of this life we've built together, that what I'm giving her isn't enough. Terrified that she's met someone else, someone who can give her the love and warmth she deserves.

A fierce surge of possessiveness that rises in me. I try to tamp down on the primal need to keep her by my side at any cost. I know I'm not an easy man to love, know I carry more baggage and scars than anyone should have to bear. Christ, my own parents abandoned me in a dumpster like yesterday's trash. Who could ever truly love a man with that kind of history?

But even as the old fears and doubts clamor in my head, I force myself to take a breath. To remember that Harper isn't like anyone else. She's kind, with a heart big enough to love even the most broken of men. If she wants to leave, I'll have to let her go. No matter how much it destroys me.

I'll do anything to persuade her to stay, to fight for this fragile, precious thing we've found together. But I won't force her, won't cage her like a bird with clipped wings. She deserves better than that. Better than me.

With a heavy heart, I rinse my mouth and leave the bathroom. I strip mechanically, my mind a million miles away. It's only when I'm down to my boxers that I realize Harper hasn't turned to watch me like she usually does. She loves to observe my little striptease, her eyes darkening with hunger as each piece of clothing falls away.

But tonight, she's facing the wall, her shoulders tense and her breathing uneven. It adds to the sinking feeling in my gut, the certainty that something is deeply wrong.

I slip into bed behind her, my hand finding hers beneath the covers. She threads our fingers together instantly, and I take a small measure of comfort in that. In the way her body still responds to mine, even if her mind is a mystery.

My lips brushing the shell of her ear.

"What's wrong, Harper? Something's been off for days."

She stiffens, her breath catching. But she doesn't pull away, and I take that as a good sign.

"You promised we'd always be honest with each other," I remind her gently. "No secrets, no holding back. I'm not great at this relationship stuff. But I'm trying. I want to be here for you, in whatever way you need. Just tell me what's going on in that beautiful head of yours."

Harper is silent for a long moment, and with each passing second, the fear in my chest grows claws and fangs. Threatening to eat me alive.

Finally, she takes a deep, shuddery breath. "I'm pregnant."

The world stops spinning. I freeze, my mind going utterly, completely blank. Pregnant. Harper is pregnant. With my child.

"I'm so sorry," she whispers, her voice thick with tears. "The birth control failed. I didn't...I didn't do this on purpose, Gabriel. I would never try to trap you like that."

Her words snap me out of my daze, and I realize with a sickening lurch that she's shaking.

"I know this isn't what you wanted," she continues, the words spilling out of her like a dam breaking. "I know you never intended to have kids. But I can't give up on these babies, Gabriel. On the lives we created together. Even if it means doing it alone. Even if it means finding another way to pay for Oscar's treatment."

She takes a deep breath, as if steeling herself. "I love you," she whispers, so softly I almost don't hear it. "I tried not to because it goes against everything we agreed to. But I couldn't help it. You mean...you mean everything to me, Gabriel."

Shock rockets through me, followed by a surge of joy. She loves me. Harper Elaine Hamilton, the woman who's become the center of my entire universe, loves me.

"You love me?" I manage, my voice hoarse and raw with emotion. "Truly?"

A tiny hiccupping sob escapes her. "I'm so sorry," she says again. "I'm sorry I ruined everything."

I'm moving before I can think, turning her in my arms until she's facing me. Until I can see the truth of her words shining in her tear-filled eyes.

"Harper!" I cup her face in my hands. "It takes two people to get pregnant. And this is a miracle!"

She blinks up at me, confusion and cautious hope warring on her face.

"But you don't want children. You were so adamant about that clause in the contract."

I take a deep breath, steeling myself to bare a truth I've never spoken aloud. "Five years ago, I had a vasectomy. I was so sure I'd never be able to be the kind of father a child deserves. So I took steps to make sure it didn't happen."

Harper blanches, her eyes going wide with shock.

"You were only thirty! God, Gabriel, that's..."

"Extreme?" I finish for her, a wry smile tugging at my lips. "Yeah. I was terrified of passing on my messed-up genes. I thought I was doing the responsible thing."

I brush my thumbs over her cheekbones, marveling at the softness of her skin. At the miracle of her, here in my arms. "I never imagined I'd meet someone like you, Harper. Someone who would make me want to reconsider everything I thought I knew about myself. About love and family and the future."

Her breath hitches, fresh tears spilling down her cheeks. "What are you saying, Gabriel?"

"I'm saying that I love you. I'm saying that I don't want to imagine my life without you. You've brought so much light and joy into my world and shown me what it means to be part of a family. If that's not love, then I don't know what is."

Her hands come up to cover mine where they cradle her face. "What about the baby? Babies, Gabriel. It's triplets."

Triplets. The word echoes in my head like a gong,

resonant and earth-shattering. Three little lives, growing even now in the woman I adore. Three tiny pieces of me and her, knit together by some inexplicable twist of fate.

Terror and wonder war in my chest, taking my breath away. I'm going to be a father. Me, the unwanted bastard who never thought he'd have a family of his own.

"We made three babies?" I choke out, awe and disbelief coloring my voice. "Harper, that's incredible."

But even as joy fills me, a lifetime of fear and self-doubt rises to meet it. I imagine all the ways I could fail them, these precious beings that are already worming their way into my heart.

"What if they inherit my messed-up leg? I wasn't exactly nurtured right. I might damage them emotionally, you know? Maybe my father was the kind of person who beat up my mother, I don't know." My hands fist in frustration. "I can't bear the thought of watching our kids suffer, Harper."

"Oh, Gabriel. Is this what you've been so afraid of? Is this why you didn't want kids?"

I nod, not trusting my voice.

"Sweetheart, listen to me. You are not your genetics. You are not your leg or your parents. You are the man I love, the man I choose every day. And you are going to be an incredible father."

A bitter laugh catching in my throat. "How can you be so sure?"

"I know how much you care, how fiercely you protect the people who matter to you. Everything you said proves how perfect you already are for this job."

I frown, not understanding. She reaches up to smooth the furrow between my brows, her touch impossibly tender.

"You're not worried about yourself, Gabriel. You're worried about our babies. About keeping them healthy and whole. And that's what makes a good father. Loving your kids, putting their needs first are the only qualifications you need."

Her words hit me like a sledgehammer, cracking open some secret, yearning place that's always longed for this - for family, for belonging. For the chance to love and be loved in return, without condition or reserve.

"It won't be easy. I'm going to fuck up and get it wrong a thousand times before I get it right."

"Of course you will. So will I. That's what parenting is. Trying and failing and trying again. But we'll do it together. You and me, and these beautiful babies we've been gifted with. We'll figure it out as we go."

Together. The word echoes in my head like a promise, like a vow more sacred than any I've ever spoken. I gather this incredible woman into my arms, burying my face in the silk of her hair as emotion overwhelms me.

"Together," I rasp, the word tasting like forever on my tongue. "God, Harper. I love you so much. I never thought I could have this."

"But you can." Her arms tighten around me. "You're an amazing man, Gabriel Cross. An amazing husband, friend and lover. And you're going to be the most wonderful dad our kids could ask for."

"Our kids. Christ, we're really having babies!"

"Three precious babies. Half you and half me and completely, totally ours."

I'm grinning like a fool now, tears streaming unchecked down my face; so fucking in love with this woman and this impossible dream made real.

"I'm going to love you, Oscar, and our three little miracles forever. I swear on everything I am that I won't take a single second for granted."

"Forever. I like the sound of that."

And then she's kissing me, long and slow and deep. Pouring all her love, all her hopes and dreams and unshakable faith into the press of her lips on mine.

And I'm kissing her back, with every shred of my battered, mending heart.

In this moment, I'm not the abandoned bastard or the boy with the scarred face and crooked leg. I'm not the closed-off billionaire or the man who thought he'd never be enough.

I'm Harper's husband. The father of her children. The man lucky enough to stand by her side, now and for all the days to come.

I'm hers in every way that matters. Just as she is mine.

CHAPTER NINE

Harper

SOMETHING IS WRONG. I felt it in the unnatural stillness of the house, the absence of Harper's usual cheerful humming as I stepped through the door after work.

I shake my head as I brush my teeth, using more force than necessary.

The past few days, she's been different. Our lovemaking has been more urgent, almost desperate, as if she's trying to pour whatever she can't say into the press of her body against mine. It's like she's slipping through my fingers, and I'm terrified of what it means.

Terrified that she's tired of me, of this life we've

built together, that what I'm giving her isn't enough. Terrified that she's met someone else, someone who can give her the love and warmth she deserves.

A fierce surge of possessiveness that rises in me. I try to tamp down on the primal need to keep her by my side at any cost. I know I'm not an easy man to love, know I carry more baggage and scars than anyone should have to bear. Christ, my own parents abandoned me in a dumpster like yesterday's trash. Who could ever truly love a man with that kind of history?

But even as the old fears and doubts clamor in my head, I force myself to take a breath. To remember that Harper isn't like anyone else. She's kind, with a heart big enough to love even the most broken of men. If she wants to leave, I'll have to let her go. No matter how much it destroys me.

I'll do anything to persuade her to stay, to fight for this fragile, precious thing we've found together. But I won't force her, won't cage her like a bird with clipped wings. She deserves better than that. Better than me.

With a heavy heart, I rinse my mouth and leave the bathroom. I strip mechanically, my mind a million miles away. It's only when I'm down to my boxers that I realize Harper hasn't turned to watch me like she usually does. She loves to observe my little striptease, her eyes darkening with hunger as each piece of clothing falls away.

But tonight, she's facing the wall, her shoulders

tense and her breathing uneven. It adds to the sinking feeling in my gut, the certainty that something is deeply wrong.

I slip into bed behind her, my hand finding hers beneath the covers. She threads our fingers together instantly, and I take a small measure of comfort in that. In the way her body still responds to mine, even if her mind is a mystery.

My lips brushing the shell of her ear.

"What's wrong, Harper? Something's been off for days."

She stiffens, her breath catching. But she doesn't pull away, and I take that as a good sign.

"You promised we'd always be honest with each other," I remind her gently. "No secrets, no holding back. I'm not great at this relationship stuff. But I'm trying. I want to be here for you, in whatever way you need. Just tell me what's going on in that beautiful head of yours."

Harper is silent for a long moment, and with each passing second, the fear in my chest grows claws and fangs. Threatening to eat me alive.

Finally, she takes a deep, shuddery breath. "I'm pregnant."

The world stops spinning. I freeze, my mind going utterly, completely blank. Pregnant. Harper is pregnant. With my child.

"I'm so sorry," she whispers, her voice thick with

tears. "The birth control failed. I didn't...I didn't do this on purpose, Gabriel. I would never try to trap you like that."

Her words snap me out of my daze, and I realize with a sickening lurch that she's shaking.

"I know this isn't what you wanted," she continues, the words spilling out of her like a dam breaking. "I know you never intended to have kids. But I can't give up on these babies, Gabriel. On the lives we created together. Even if it means doing it alone. Even if it means finding another way to pay for Oscar's treatment."

She takes a deep breath, as if steeling herself. "I love you," she whispers, so softly I almost don't hear it. "I tried not to because it goes against everything we agreed to. But I couldn't help it. You mean...you mean everything to me, Gabriel."

Shock rockets through me, followed by a surge of joy. She loves me. Harper Elaine Hamilton, the woman who's become the center of my entire universe, loves me.

"You love me?" I manage, my voice hoarse and raw with emotion. "Truly?"

A tiny hiccupping sob escapes her. "I'm so sorry," she says again. "I'm sorry I ruined everything."

I'm moving before I can think, turning her in my arms until she's facing me. Until I can see the truth of her words shining in her tear-filled eyes.

"Harper!" I cup her face in my hands. "It takes two

people to get pregnant. And this is a miracle!"

She blinks up at me, confusion and cautious hope warring on her face.

"But you don't want children. You were so adamant about that clause in the contract."

I take a deep breath, steeling myself to bare a truth I've never spoken aloud. "Five years ago, I had a vasectomy. I was so sure I'd never be able to be the kind of father a child deserves. So I took steps to make sure it didn't happen."

Harper blanches, her eyes going wide with shock.

"You were only thirty! God, Gabriel, that's..."

"Extreme?" I finish for her, a wry smile tugging at my lips. "Yeah. I was terrified of passing on my messed-up genes. I thought I was doing the responsible thing."

I brush my thumbs over her cheekbones, marveling at the softness of her skin. At the miracle of her, here in my arms. "I never imagined I'd meet someone like you, Harper. Someone who would make me want to reconsider everything I thought I knew about myself. About love and family and the future."

Her breath hitches, fresh tears spilling down her cheeks. "What are you saying, Gabriel?"

"I'm saying that I love you. I'm saying that I don't want to imagine my life without you. You've brought so much light and joy into my world and shown me what it means to be part of a family. If that's not love, then I don't know what is."

Her hands come up to cover mine where they cradle

her face. "What about the baby? Babies, Gabriel. It's triplets."

Triplets. The word echoes in my head like a gong, resonant and earth-shattering. Three little lives, growing even now in the woman I adore. Three tiny pieces of me and her, knit together by some inexplicable twist of fate.

Terror and wonder war in my chest, taking my breath away. I'm going to be a father. Me, the unwanted bastard who never thought he'd have a family of his own.

"We made three babies?" I choke out, awe and disbelief coloring my voice. "Harper, that's incredible."

But even as joy fills me, a lifetime of fear and self-doubt rises to meet it. I imagine all the ways I could fail them, these precious beings that are already worming their way into my heart.

"What if they inherit my messed-up leg? I wasn't exactly nurtured right. I might damage them emotionally, you know? Maybe my father was the kind of person who beat up my mother, I don't know." My hands fist in frustration. "I can't bear the thought of watching our kids suffer, Harper."

"Oh, Gabriel. Is this what you've been so afraid of? Is this why you didn't want kids?"

I nod, not trusting my voice.

"Sweetheart, listen to me. You are not your genetics. You are not your leg or your parents. You are the man I love, the man I choose every day. And you are going to be an incredible father."

A bitter laugh catching in my throat. "How can you be so sure?"

"I know how much you care, how fiercely you protect the people who matter to you. Everything you said proves how perfect you already are for this job."

I frown, not understanding. She reaches up to smooth the furrow between my brows, her touch impossibly tender.

"You're not worried about yourself, Gabriel. You're worried about our babies. About keeping them healthy and whole. And that's what makes a good father. Loving your kids, putting their needs first are the only qualifications you need."

Her words hit me like a sledgehammer, cracking open some secret, yearning place that's always longed for this - for family, for belonging. For the chance to love and be loved in return, without condition or reserve.

"It won't be easy. I'm going to fuck up and get it wrong a thousand times before I get it right."

"Of course you will. So will I. That's what parenting is. Trying and failing and trying again. But we'll do it together. You and me, and these beautiful babies we've been gifted with. We'll figure it out as we go."

Together. The word echoes in my head like a promise, like a vow more sacred than any I've ever spoken. I gather this incredible woman into my arms, burying my face in the silk of her hair as emotion overwhelms me.

"Together," I rasp, the word tasting like forever on my tongue. "God, Harper. I love you so much. I never thought I could have this."

"But you can." Her arms tighten around me. "You're an amazing man, Gabriel Cross. An amazing husband, friend and lover. And you're going to be the most wonderful dad our kids could ask for."

"Our kids. Christ, we're really having babies!"

"Three precious babies. Half you and half me and completely, totally ours."

I'm grinning like a fool now, tears streaming unchecked down my face; so fucking in love with this woman and this impossible dream made real.

"I'm going to love you, Oscar, and our three little miracles forever. I swear on everything I am that I won't take a single second for granted."

"Forever. I like the sound of that."

And then she's kissing me, long and slow and deep. Pouring all her love, all her hopes and dreams and unshakable faith into the press of her lips on mine.

And I'm kissing her back, with every shred of my battered, mending heart.

In this moment, I'm not the abandoned bastard or the boy with the scarred face and crooked leg. I'm not the closed-off billionaire or the man who thought he'd never be enough.

I'm Harper's husband. The father of her children. The man lucky enough to stand by her side, now and for all the days to come.

I'm hers in every way that matters. Just as she is mine.

EPILOGUE

Gabriel

Seven Years Later

I SMILE AS our six-year-old kids help me and Harper finish setting up our tents for the night. The air is crisp and clean, filled with the sweet scent of pine and the distant chirping of birds. It's peaceful out here, a welcome respite from the bustling chaos of the city.

Oscar and his girlfriend, Sarah, have just finished pitching their own tent a few yards away. They're laughing together as they work, their easy camaraderie bringing a smile to my face. It's still a little surreal sometimes, seeing Oscar all grown up and in love.

Harper glances over at them, her expression soft with affection. She comes to stand beside me as the kids explore the tents. "Sarah brings out the best in him."

I slip an arm around her waist and tug her close. "And he adores her; anyone can see that."

Harper leans into me, rests her head on my

shoulder. "I'm so happy for him."

"We should start thinking about renovating the annex at home. In case they want a place of their own someday."

"You'd be okay with that?"

"Oscar is family, Harper. And family sticks together. If living in the annex gives them the independence they need while still keeping them close, I'm all for it."

She stretches up to kiss me, her lips soft and sweet against mine.

"With a little support, they can have a happy life together. Sarah's mom has always been very protective of her, even when Sarah and Oscar were at school. She's worried about Sarah dating. If they decide to marry, I think the fact they are staying with us will reassure her."

She rests her head on my shoulder again and we stay like that for a long moment, our kid's laughter surrounding us.

"Mom and Dad would have loved seeing Oscar healthy and happy, and us all together like this. Camping was their favorite family tradition."

I tighten my arms around her, offering silent comfort. I know how much she misses her parents, how bittersweet these moments can be without them.

"They'd be so proud of you. Of the amazing woman and mother you are. They'd be bursting with pride at how well you've loved Oscar, how you've given him a full, joyful life."

A single tear slips down her cheek, and I brush it

away tenderly. "Sometimes, I can't believe he only needs check-ups once a year."

"You made that happen, Harper." I turn her face to mine. "Your love, your dedication...that's what got him here. Never forget that."

She leans into my touch, turning her head to press a kiss to my palm. And then the kids are bounding over, their little faces alight with excitement, and the moment is broken.

But the warmth of it lingers, a constant glow in my chest as we spend the afternoon exploring the campsite together. Harper and I take turns pointing out different plants and animals to the triplets, watching their eyes go wide with wonder at every new discovery.

Ethan, our little thrill-seeker, wants to climb every tree and splash in every puddle. Our budding artist, Destiny, keeps stopping to collect leaves and flowers to press into her sketchbook later. And Ava, our quiet dreamer, is content to hold my hand and take it all in with those big, thoughtful eyes that are so much like her mother's.

I'm in awe of them, these perfect little beings we created. They're the best parts of Harper and me.

As the sun dips towards the horizon, we make our way back to the campsite to start dinner. Oscar and Sarah have already got a fire going, the flickering flames casting a warm, inviting glow over the clearing.

I watch Harper as she moves around the campsite, her movements graceful and sure as she unpacks the food and dishes out graham crackers and chocolate for s'mores. She's beautiful in the golden light, her skin glowing and her eyes sparkling with contentment.

Even now, after years of marriage and three kids, she still takes my breath away. Still makes my heart race and my palms sweat like a teenager with his first crush.

I know I'm a lucky man. I have a wife who loves me, children who bring me joy and a brother-in-law who's become a true sibling. And now, with Sarah, our little family feels complete.

It's not always perfect, of course. We have our difficulties like anyone else. There are days when the kids drive us crazy, when Harper and I butt heads over parenting styles.

I'm still learning, still growing. I make mistakes, spoil the kids a bit too much sometimes. Harper has to be the disciplinarian more often than not, reining us all in with that firm but loving touch that comes so naturally to her.

But we're in it together, every step of the way. We've built a life on a foundation of love and trust and unshakable commitment, and that's what sees us through the tough times.

And the good times. God, the good times make it all worthwhile.

Moments like this one, with my family all around me. With laughter ringing out through the trees and the sweet scent of chocolate and marshmallows mingling with the wood smoke. With Harper by my side, her hand in mine and her love wrapped around my heart like a promise.

After the start I had in life, I thought I was incapable of giving or receiving love. Harper showed me differently. She saw the man I could be, the father and husband and friend.

And slowly, day by day, I started to heal. There are still times when the old fears and doubts creep in, when I question whether I'm good enough, whether I deserve this much happiness.

But then I look at Harper, at our kids. I see the love shining in their eyes, the trust and adoration. And I know I am enough. That I'm exactly where I'm meant to be.

That this beautiful, imperfectly perfect life is everything.

And I wouldn't trade a single second of it for anything in the world.

The End

MARRYING THE PROTECTIVE PROFESSOR

CURVY BRIDES OF BLOSSOM FORD #1

August

ALL MY LIFE I've secretly wished I was born and raised in an ordinary family, with loving, welcoming parents instead of being the town's sign of bad luck, growing up at Blossom Ford Orphanage and having the town's name as my surname, like the other kids there. I can't help believing if I was wanted, the acceptance and sense of belonging would have helped me become someone who knows how to love. That belief is strongest when I think of Ella Mitchell.

It's Friday night so ensuring she gets home safely is my top priority as I park my SUV a short distance from Jackson's Diner where she's working, far enough to see the door of the restaurant but not so close that anyone might link my presence to the diner. I don't care how the interfering residents of Blossom Ford view me, but I don't want rumors to spread about Ella.

I slide down the car seat, getting comfortable even as I curse myself for the warmth that spreads through my chest at the mere thought of her name. As I've done a millionth time, I tell myself I'm here to protect her.

An uncomfortable tightness in my chest and a bitter taste in my mouth that I'm all too familiar with have me exhaling slowly. But it's hard to chase away the guilt. I cannot keep from committing the same sin. I'm a scarred, divorced, grizzly mountain of a man that's old enough to be her father while she's a beautiful, innocent twenty-two-year-old with her whole life ahead of her. Ella deserves better than me. But I still can't stop thinking about her.

It makes no difference that what I feel for her is more than physical attraction. I love her strength, soft smile and the way she's warm to everyone that crosses paths with her. There's a certainty in my bones that she's meant for me alone. This only makes the guilt worse. I should let her go because I love her.

And I have. To a point. For the last two years since I returned to Blossom Ford, saw her for the first time and fell for the kindness in her honey hued eyes and the sweetest curves I'd ever seen, I've stopped myself from approaching her. From claiming her. At least in real life. Because in my dreams, I've made love to her every single night and spent my days laughing with her. I've always considered my self-control one of my strongest attributes, but I can't stop dreaming about her.

I can't help the fact that I won't have her driving home by herself at midnight, after her shifts at the diner on Fridays and Saturdays. If I'm an asshole, so be it. And if deep down I know as well as ensuring she's safe, I have to see her face, I'll take the guilt and deal with it.

I frown when only two cars remain in the parking lot. One is old Jackson's beat up truck, and the other belongs to Rosie; the woman who works with Ella. Ella's old yellow mini should be right besides Rosie's.

The door to the diner flies open and Rosie marches out in her apron, phone glued to her ear. She sprints to her car. My frown thickens. How is Ella going to get home? Will she be closing on her own? I force myself to stay in the car. As much as I want to rush in and help, keeping a distance is crucial to my self-discipline.

I ramp up the air conditioning in the car a little higher. It usually takes one hour to close, but tonight, it'll take Ella longer. Old Jackson doesn't think hard work hurts women. There's no way he's going to help with setting the dinner to the way he likes it.

I keep my eyes on the door and an hour and a half later, I'm rewarded with the sight of Ella's curvy hips wrapped in hugging denim and the soft way her breasts hug her blouse. Even after a ten-hour shift, she's a vision that gets my heart racing.

She zeroes in on my car and it's like she can see me, like she knows I'm waiting here for her. She does this on Fridays and Saturdays; the days I wait for her. If she worked any other nights, I'd wait for her then, too. She's friends with Mrs. Gallagher, the orphanage director who's the closest thing to a mother I've ever had. Ella must think of me as a much older brother who's looking out for her.

She steps on the street and heads towards me. I know that she's just taking the road to her house, but I can't stop my heart from beating even faster. It's like this every time I see her.

I'm feeling something else too; anger. Her walking alone down the empty street at this time of the night is pissing me off.

She's only a few feet from me when a car careens down the street and stops beside her. I sit up straight, hoping a friend is coming to pick her up. But she doesn't slow down, even after spotting the car.

I scowl as a man stumbles out of the car and steps in her path. It's Toby Anderson, Ella's ex. Something ugly rears in me. Despite my unstoppable feelings for Ella, whenever I see him, I realize how great my self-control is. Every time I saw him with Ella, I wanted to knock him out. The four months they dated were an exercise in self-discipline I didn't think I was going to win. But for Ella, to give her the chance at happiness she deserved with someone her age that could give her a comfortable life, I held myself back.

I don't like the way Toby sways on his feet. The light from the full moon and lamppost in front of the diner are enough to make out the disgust on Ella's face.

Before I know it, my hand is on the door handle, but my eyes don't stray from Toby.

They are talking but the loud music and shouts from the car stop me from hearing what they are saying. Toby reaches out a hand and touches Ella's arm. She wrenches it back.

I'm out of the car. I sprint towards them, her safety the only thought in my mind. for her, I'd tried staying away, but her safety is something I'll not compromise on. even if it means she might hate me for interfering with her life.

FAKE MARRYING THE BODYGUARD

THE O'CONNORS OF BLOSSOM FORD #4

Bonnie

I KEEP MY eyes tightly shut and listen for noises around me. It's too quiet. I'm used to the sounds of cars honking, people going about the apartment. Then a sudden high sound startles me and I grab the bed sheet. I take a while to work out it's a bird call.

When my heart settles, I can tell I'm alone. I know the feeling of being watched all too well; this isn't it. I allow myself to open my eyes and stare around an unfamiliar, semi dark room. Instead of white stone walls and marble floors, there are wooden walls and floors.

My breath hitches when I notice the large window opposite me. The sun is setting and the deep orange and pink colors inside the golden ball are breathtaking. There are trees outside with some of their leaves turning a burnt orange; it's a mesmerizing depiction of fall. A little while later, I realize I'm still staring and pull myself up on it.

I don't know where I am, so why am I admiring the view? I'm usually so vigilant about my environment. Have I finally gone mad, like Dad always said I would one day?

I shake my head. I move the soft bed sheet aside and look down at my body, taking in the white dress.

Memories of Rory, the wedding and escaping the life I lived for twenty years return.

I must have fallen asleep on the way here. This must be his cabin.

A soft knock sounds. My eyes shift to the door. Heart pounding, I tumble out of the massive bed and stand. I try to answer, but no sound comes out of my mouth. I clear my throat and try again, using all my acting skills to strengthen my voice.

"Yes?" There's no sign of the nerves trying to strangle my throat. I hide my trembling hands behind my back.

"It's Rory. Can I open the door?"

Even if he hadn't identified himself, I would have known it was him. There was something unique about the lilting rhythm of his deep voice. It made me want to relax around him, want to trust him.

When I say yes, he opens the door but doesn't leg to of it. Light enters the room, allowing me to see the way his sea-green eyes rove over me before they return to my face. Some of the tension leaves me. His gaze is familiar, he's looked at me like that countless times in the year he's guarded me.

What's different is his attire. I've never seen him in anything other than a white shirt and dark suit. He's wearing a t-shirt that outlines his muscles and low hanging blue jeans. My heart skips a beat and this time it has nothing to do with nerves. His auburn hair is wet, as if he's just come out of a shower. He looks younger than his forty-one years. More approachable. I swallow, struggling with my unsuitable and unwanted attraction to this man, who just happens to be my husband.

"Dinner is ready. Come have a bite, lass."

Why does it feel like he's showering me with affection whenever he calls me by that word? I can feel my nose crinkle as I try to stare him down, to figure out why he used that word. He stares back blankly, then shuts the door, leaving me in semidarkness again.

I bring my hands in front of me. Even though my heart is still racing and my body feels alive, my fingers are steady. I'm attracted to but not scared of him.

Can I really trust Rory the way my body seems to believe it can? Or have I escaped from my controlling father only to fall into the hands of a more wicked monster?

I didn't always feel like I could trust Rory. Dad contracted his personal bodyguard services firm after the company he previously used failed to catch my stalker for three years. The stalker had become more dangerous, nearly kidnapped me once.

That's when Dad brought Rory in, even though he seemed to have reservations about hiring the ex-Mixed Martial Arts athlete. I'd never understood that. The Red King, as Rory was called by those in the sport, was Dad's favorite fighter. Now, maybe I do. He seems decent, somehow different from Dad.

The men that guarded me were also my jailors. I'd learned the hard way that all the workers in the house, no matter their position, were Dad's people. Rory terrified me the most. First, for the same reason Dad loved the MMA fighter. His explosive, merciless fighting style. It made me think he was cruel. The other reason was scarier. For the first time in seven years, I was behaving like a high school girl with a severe crush. I did my damnedest to hide my growing attraction.

But only three months later, his security team caught the stalker when he attempted to kidnap me again. Rory's powerful arms had held me against the strong column of his chest and stroked my damp hair.

"You're safe, lass," he'd said softly, emotion lacing his voice as if he really cared about me.

I told myself he was doing his job, that he was the type of competitive person who had to always win and the emotion in that ragged, comforting voice of his was pride. However, since then, it became almost impossible to hide my attraction. Worse, I'm developing feelings for him.

The way he interacted with me didn't change but I

began putting a different meaning to his cryptic once overs when he started a shift. I couldn't shake the feeling he was checking to see if I was alright.

After watching him for six months since the stalking incident, I worked up the courage to ask him for help. I had to escape from Dad. My life had become a survival game long ago, and I was exhausted from living that way. I sang and smiled for crowds, but I'd lost my passion for singing, the only thing that gave me joy for so long.

To the public, I was a bubbly singer with millions of fans, but my private life comprised long hours of practice, rigorous diets and exercises imposed by Dad. I had tried escaping once, only to be brought back by one of my so-called bodyguards. He controlled my fortune and made decisions about my welfare. My will to live was disappearing at the thought of having to live that way for the rest of my life.

One day, while I was out doing the exercises Dad insisted on, I pretended to fall. When Rory helped me up, I explained how Dad was blackmailing me with two videos he took of me thrashing his study when I was seventeen and twenty-one. He was threatening to have me put under a conservatorship. I have no memory of vandalizing his study, but it was me in those videos. I suspected Dad drugged me, but had no way of proving that.

I was ready to give him all my fortune if he could help me flee. If he will enter a temporary marriage contract with me, before Dad got wind of anything, it'd be extremely hard to impose a conservatorship when I had a spouse willing to testify my mental capacity was sound. Especially if it was someone as influential as Rory.

"What if I do the same thing your dad is doing? I could keep your money and control you the way he does," Rory had asked, sea-green eyes steady on mine, as he crouched beside me on the green grass of the park.

It was the start of summer and a hot day but I went ice cold. I'd searched his face, lack of trust in my ability to judge people strong. Since the age of five, I grew up with Dad telling me people couldn't be trusted, that they didn't care for me. The only thing they loved was my voice and the smiling singer Bonnie. Maybe I was wrong about Rory.

I'd strengthened my back, focused on his steady gaze.

"I won't carry on the way I am."

"Okay, lass. I'll draft the papers. The only way to make sure you're permanently safe is to get those files, anything else he might have, and find something on him to make him believe if he ever tries to control you again, he'll be ruined."

"Is that possible?" My heart was in my mouth.

"Nothing is impossible where humans are concerned."

It took Rory three months to get everything sorted. Three long months of hope and fear. Usually, Dad left me alone, trusting in the army of people he'd placed around me to report my daily life. We had lunch together once a month at his favorite restaurant. I thought he'd see something was up, that I'd mustered the courage to flee. When he suspected nothing, I was so thankful he'd forced me to take acting classes.

Rory and his team found out Dad was involved with an organized crime ring of underage prostitution. A friend of his married us before Rory threatened Dad with providing proof of his illegal activities to the police if he ever tried to force me back to him.

I switch on the bedside lamp and gaze around the room. My one suitcase and guitar are under the window. I remove a flowing maxi dress and run my fingers through the soft fabric. It's one of the few dresses I'd hidden from Dad.

No matter how much he controlled my diet and exercises, my chubbiness never went away. His solution, which never really worked, was to have me wear body-shaping outfits at home, too. For a while now, I have hoped to wear maxi dresses whenever I wanted.

I get clean underwear and toiletries. I'm a little fazed that there's no ensuite in the bedroom, but I shake it off. Compared to the fact I might live life my way, it's only a minute drawback.

Rory's standing by the sink when I open the door. I was quiet but he must have heard, because he turns around. He's wearing a white apron knitted with a large picture of one of the Sesame Street characters. It covers almost all the apron.

A chuckle comes out of me before I can stop myself.

"Something funny?" His face is impassive.

It only causes me to crack up again. I cover my mouth with my free hand, unsure of what to say. My eyes refuse to move away from the knitted character. It looks so alive.

"My Mom and Aunt Caitlin made this apron especially for me. It's one of my favorites."

"It's beautiful. I mean, it looks good on you."

His lips lift.

My hands tighten on my clothes. Because I've just gone from humor to heat in a heartbeat. My cheeks flush. I can't drag my eyes away from that sexy face of his. I've never seen Rory smile like this. Like he doesn't have a care in the world, like an innocent boy.

"Do you mean it?" He asks.

"Mean what?"

"This overall looks good on me."

Did his eyes darken? He's no longer smiling, but I'm not exactly worried. Something about the way he's watching me is putting my body on alert. A panty melting kind of alert.

"Where's the bathroom?" I ask, unsure of what the tension between us means.

He points to a closed door and I dash in, locking the door. I wash and dress slowly, going over our conversation again and again, but I can't work out the meaning behind the expression in his eyes.

I give myself a stern lecture before I exit the bathroom. I've just left one prison. My body may feel Rory is safe, but I don't know him well.

Right now, Dad is petrified of what Rory might do, so sticking to him gives me the best protection against being dragged back to my old life. However, still I have to be careful of Rory and any people I meet.

Even if Rory has no evil intentions towards me, I still must keep myself from falling further for him. No matter how much I wish he were truly in love with me and wanted to spend the rest of his life with me, it's not likely to happen. What could a successful, ruggedly handsome man in his prime like Rory, want with an insecure, inexperienced, chubby woman like me, when he has the world's most beautiful women vying for his attention?

OTHER BOOKS BY THE AUTHOR

CURVY BRIDES OF BLOSSOM FORD SERIES

MARRYING THE PROTECTIVE PROFESSOR

MARRYING THE GRUMPY DIRECTOR

MARRYING THE POSSESSIVE NEIGHBOR

MARRYING THE WIDOWED DOCTOR

MARRYING THE SCARRED SOLDIER

MARRYING THE OBSESSIVE CEO

MARRYING THE BIG MOUNTAIN MAN

THE O'CONNORS OF BLOSSOM FORD SERIES

MATCHED TO PATRICK

REDEEMING THE MOUNTAIN MAN

BROTHER'S BEST FRIEND OBSESSION

FAKE MARRYING THE BODYGUARD

A FLING FOR CHRISTMAS

SINGLE DAD'S CHRISTMAS GIFT

SNOWED IN WITH THE SILVER FOX

FOREVER YOUR BEST FRIEND

MAKE ME YOURS AGAIN

ABOUT THE AUTHOR

Iris West writes short and spicy romance about alpha heroes and the women they can't help falling in love with. She loves reading all types of romance books that have a happy ending and is an avid Kdrama fan.

Follow or like her on Facebook, Instagram Tik Tok and/or Goodreads.

FREE BOOK

Would you like a free book? Sign up to my mailing list at https://dl.bookfunnel.com/t191w45ryj to receive a copy of Loving My Fake Husband, a Curvy Brides of Blossom Ford short story.

HELP OTHERS FIND THIS BOOK

Thank you for reading His Convenient Curvy Bride. If you enjoyed this book, please help others discover it by leaving a review at your favorite online bookstore.

Many thanks,

Iris xx